Hector the Collector

EMILY BEENY

Illustrated by STEPHANIE GRAEGIN

ROARING BROOK PRESS   New York

It all begin with an acorn.

It was smooth and brown with a rough, knobbly cap, and Hector found it in a crack in the sidewalk on the way to school.

At recess, he found two more.

One was skinny and green.

The other was short and
chubby, like an old man with
his hat pulled over his eyes.

On the way home, he picked up some more.

Two were as green as apples.

Two were brown and grainy like wood.

One was golden and smooth like polished stone.

Some were round.
Some were long.
Some were stubby.

They all had rough,
knobbly caps.

They were all different.

They were all the same.

They were all beautiful.

Every week there were more.

Hector put them in his pockets,
and when his pockets were full,
he put them in his desk at school.

One day after lunch, his teacher checked
everyone's desk to see if they were all tidy.

Everyone else had pencils and notebooks.

Hector's was the only desk full of acorns.

Everyone laughed.

"Where are your pencils?"
asked Alex.

"Where are your pens?"
asked Evan.

"What are you doing with all
those acorns?" asked André.

"Maybe he's a squirrel!"
shouted Maddie.

Hector was so embarrassed.

But their teacher said, "Hector isn't a squirrel. He's a collector. I bet he had a good reason for choosing each of these."

"Well," Hector said slowly, and began to show them one by one.

"This one is gold. And this one is green."
His classmates all moved closer to see.

"These ones are short and fat."
Everyone giggled.

"This one is tall and skinny."
Everyone looked.

"They're all different,

and they're all the same,

and they're all beautiful."

Everyone was quiet.

"That," said the teacher,
"is what makes a great collection.
I bet some of you have collections, too."

Slowly, Alex raised her hand.

She collected pennies in a jar.

And Evan collected
stuffed animals.

André collected fortune-cookie fortunes.

And Maddie collected smoothed-down glass from the beach. It was called sea glass.

Jesse's father collected baseball cards.

And Derek's grandma
collected stamps.

There were lots of ways to collect things.

You could collect old scraps of fabric in a quilt.

Or photographs in an album.

Or songs in your head.

Some collections took up a whole building.

Like the Museum of Natural History,

where they collected butterflies
and bones.

Or the Public Library,

where they collected books.

Or the Metropolitan Museum,

where they collected paintings and sculptures from all over the world and from all of time.

Those collections belonged to everyone.

But some collections, like Hector's,
belonged to just one person.

Every collection was
different.

Every collection
was the same.

Every collection was beautiful.

Author's Note

Almost everyone collects something. Bottle caps or comic books, seashells or seedpods, paintings or paper clips, books or beads. A collection contains things that are beautiful or interesting or strange, things that we find scattered out in the world but that seem to us to belong together.

Collections can be **private** or **public**, secret or famous. They can fill a paper bag, a room, or a whole museum. I love collections, big and small. I've collected postcards and sea glass and fortune-cookie fortunes, and as a curator I've also helped museums collect and care for works of art made hundreds of years ago. To me, what's most special about a **museum** is that it's where things that used to belong to one person come to belong to everyone, where we can all go to see, enjoy, and learn from many kinds of collections.

The **Musée du Louvre**, for example, is a famous museum in Paris, France. Its collections—hundreds and hundreds of paintings and sculptures and tapestries and treasures—once belonged to French kings. Today, these things belong to the French people, and millions of visitors see them every year.

The Louvre takes up a giant palace, but the **Frick Collection**, a museum in New York City, fits into a house. At the beginning of the last century, that house belonged to Henry Clay Frick, a collector who wanted to share his favorite things with the public. Now, visitors can walk through his living room, his dining room, his library, and his garden, enjoying the paintings, sculptures, and furniture that Mr. Frick loved.

The Frick Collection and the Louvre are both **art museums**, places where man-made objects have been chosen for their beauty and their significance to the history of art. There are many art museums around the world, from Boston to Buenos Aires, from St. Louis to Sydney. They show paintings and sculptures, prints and drawings, photographs and videos, furniture, costumes, jewelry, and even ancient Egyptian mummies. Art museums are my favorite, but there are lots of other kinds of interesting museums.

At **natural history museums**, for example, you can see collections of plants, rocks, animals, and fossils: objects that tell the story of the natural world and the place of humans in it. At the **George C. Page Museum** in Los Angeles, you can see the skeletons of saber-toothed tigers that were preserved more than 11,000 years ago in a pit of tar. At the Smithsonian's **National Museum of Natural History** in Washington, D.C., you can see a famous blue rock called the Hope Diamond.

History museums tell the story of a person, a place, or a moment in time. At the **New York Transit Museum**, there are subway trains, tokens, and turnstiles on display.

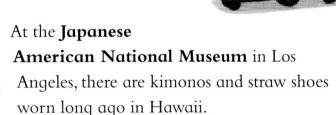

At the **Japanese American National Museum** in Los Angeles, there are kimonos and straw shoes worn long ago in Hawaii.

Every collection tells a story about the things in it, and about the person or people who brought those things together.

Every collection is different.

Every collection is the same.

Just like all of us.

For Abe, who collected baseball cards,
and for Clare, who collected stickers
—E.B.

For Gloria, who collects beautiful things
—S.G.

Text copyright © 2017 by Emily Beeny
Illustrations copyright © 2017 by Stephanie Graegin
Published by Roaring Brook Press
Roaring Brook Press is a division of Holtzbrinck Publishing Holdings Limited Partnership
175 Fifth Avenue, New York, New York 10010

mackids.com

Library of Congress Cataloging-in-Publication Data

Names: Beeny, Emily A., author. | Graegin, Stephanie, illustrator.
Title: Hector the collector / by Emily Beeny ; illustrated by Stephanie
    Graegin.
Description: First edition. | New York : Roaring Brook Press, 2017. |
    Summary: Hector begins collecting acorns of different sizes and shapes and
    is teased about it when his classmates find out, until their teacher
    explains about collections and asks who else has one. Includes author's
    note about various kinds of collections.
Identifiers: LCCN 2016038251 | ISBN 9781626722965 (hardcover)
Subjects: | CYAC: Collectors and collecting—Fiction. | Acorns—Fiction. |
    Schools—Fiction. | Animals—Fiction. | BISAC: JUVENILE FICTION / Animals
    / General. | JUVENILE FICTION / Nature & the Natural World / General (see
    also headings under Animals). | JUVENILE FICTION / Social Issues /
    Bullying.
Classification: LCC PZ7.1.B4434 Hec 2017 | DDC [E]—dc23
LC record available at https://lccn.loc.gov/2016038251

Our books may be purchased in bulk for promotional, educational, or business use.
Please contact your local bookseller or the Macmillan Corporate and Premium Sales Department
at (800) 221-7945 ext. 5442 or by e-mail at MacmillanSpecialMarkets@macmillan.com.

First edition, 2017
Book design by Roberta Pressel
Printed in China by RR Donnelley Asia Printing Solutions Ltd.,
Dongguan City, Guangdong Province

1 3 5 7 9 10 8 6 4 2